SNOW!

by Christine Ford
pictures by Candace Whitman

 HarperFestival®

A Division of HarperCollins*Publishers*

Tug tug
hats and gloves

Zipper up
snowsuit snug

Go go
kick up snow

Snowflakes cold flakes
blow blow blow

Puppy races
chases tags

Yum yum
snowflake crumbs

Melt so quickly
on our tongues

Slide slide
down we glide

Swish swoosh
goes our ride

Pack pack
pile stack

Toss a snowball
get one back

Tap tap
snowman's cap

Twist a scarf
wrap wrap wrap

Cherry cheeks
sleds in tow